FOOTBALL MAD

"Pass it back!" Danny yelled.

Out of the corner of his eye, Gary saw all three Eastfields' forwards crowding in on him. He had no room for manoeuvre. A throw-in was out of the question now, and he didn't want to give away a corner.

"TO ME!" he heard Danny screaming.

Finally, Gary had to admit that he had no other choice. Three against one was too much. He looked up, nodded at Danny and toe-punted the ball gently towards him.

At least, that's what he meant to do.

Chapter 1

"To me, to me, to me!" yelled Craig as Gary took control of the ball.

But as always, Gary Connell was trying to be too clever. With less than three minutes left of the match, this was dangerous. There was too much at stake. The score was 2-1 to St Botolph's, but if they wanted to stay ahead – and win the cup – they needed to hold on and play safe.

As Craig watched the sea of red shirts bearing down on the goal area, his heart began to pound. It was already too late for Gary to pass.

"Kick it back!" he shouted. "Back to Danny."

Danny Thompson stood in the goal watching Gary with growing unease. Why didn't he just clear the ball?

"Get rid of it!" he screamed.

But Gary had got himself boxed in. He glanced up at the two red-shirted players speeding towards him.

"Piece of cake!" he muttered, as he dribbled the ball slowly forwards.

He managed to wrong-foot their number 4, and slipped it past the number 2.

Magic! he thought to himself.

But then, disaster! Before Gary could kick it away, their number 7 appeared from nowhere. He managed to get his toe to the ball. Gary watched in horror as it skidded out of his control.

Now things were really serious. In desperation, Gary lunged forward. He just managed to back-kick the ball.

Unfortunately, the number 4 was waiting behind him. Keeping his head, Gary spun around and skilfully dribbled the ball past him.

"Pass it back!" Danny yelled.

Out of the corner of his eye, Gary saw all three Eastfields forwards crowding in on him. He had no room for manoeuvre. A throw-in was out of the question now, and he didn't want to give away a corner.

"TO ME!" he heard Danny screaming.

Finally, Gary had to admit that he had no other choice. He was good, but not *that* good! Three against one was too much. He looked up, nodded at Danny and toe-punted the ball gently towards him.

At least, that's what he meant to do.

Perhaps it was the pressure which made him overreact, perhaps the wind caught the ball, or perhaps, as Eastfields' number 2 claimed, he'd managed to get a boot to it himself. Whatever. As players and spectators looked on, the ball whistled over Danny's outstretched arms, hit the nearside post and rebounded into the net.

The next moment the ref blew the final whistle. It was all over.

"You idiot," Craig groaned, but his words were drowned out by the cheers of the rival team and its supporters. Saved from almost certain defeat, they were going wild. The final score was a sickening two-all draw. There would have to be a replay – the return match to be held away at Eastfields.

With their heads down, the boys of St Botolph's made their way to the changing rooms. So near, yet so far. And all because of Gary Connell! As Luke Edwards walked past, he paused, and slapped Gary on the back.

"Nice one," he hissed.

"Yeah," Maurice Meacham jeered. "Brilliant goal. *Captain*."

"Perhaps it's time we had a new captain," Wesley Hunter added, and a disgruntled murmur of agreement went round the rest of the team.

Gary had let everyone down. He felt sick.

Chapter 2

Craig Taggart. Danny Thompson. Gary Connell. The three of them were the best of mates. They wore the same brand of trainers, they rode the same make of bike, they listened to the same kind of music on their identical Walkmans. They all liked computer games, cheeseburgers and ketchup; they all disliked books, girls and any vegetable which happened to be green. Their passion was football.

Every evening after school – winter and summer, rain and shine – they would meet up over the rec. At the far end, someone had painted goalposts on the wall of the bus station which backed on to the park. It was here that the three of them spent hours playing Corner.

Taking it in turns, Craig, then Gary, would float the ball over towards the goal, while the other attempted to head it past Danny. It was a simple enough game, but one they never tired of. In fact, if it hadn't been for school, they might have spent their entire lives there.

Sadly for them there *was* school. Six hours a day's worth, five days a week! Time when they couldn't play football. Time when they couldn't even discuss tactics. For although they were all in the same class, Miss MacDonald had learnt early on in the term that it was best to keep the three of them apart. She had sent Craig and Danny to opposite sides of the room, while Gary – whom she suspected was the ringleader – was placed in the middle of the front row.

"Where I can keep an eye on you," she'd said.

As far as Craig, Danny and Gary were concerned, the only good thing about school was the football team. At the beginning of the year, Danny had proposed and Craig had seconded Gary as captain. Since taking over, he'd steered the team to the top of the local league and into the cup final. As the game had got nearer, everyone had been dreaming of winning the cup.

For the time being at least, that dream was over.

Since they all lived on the same estate, the three of them usually went to school and – if none of them had been kept behind for misbehaving – returned home together. But that afternoon was different.

Gary's antics on the football pitch had pushed their friendship to the limit.

Scoring an own-goal was the ultimate disgrace. After he had showered, Gary Connell made his way home alone.

"If I could just have jumped a bit higher," Danny said miserably.

Craig shook his head. "There was no way," he said.

"I feel so rotten!" Danny muttered.

"It wasn't *your* fault!" said Craig. "It was Gary. The idiot! Always trying to be so flash!"

The boys walked on in silence. Past the shops, past the boarded-up cinema, over the level crossing.

"It was a pretty good goal he scored in the first half," said Danny finally.

"Yeah, great," said Craig. "Only that doesn't give him the right to throw it all away in the second half." He kicked at a stone, which went bouncing over the pavement and into the road. "Two-all!" he yelled. "Two-pigging-two!"

As they reached the edge of the estate, Danny looked up.

"Fancy going up the rec later?" he said.

"No," said Craig. "Not tonight."

Danny shook his head. "Me neither," he said. "Do you think Banana Brain will turn up?"

Craig shrugged. "Who knows?" he said. "Who cares?"

Chapter 3

Gary felt truly awful – worse even than when his dog, Striker, had got run over. For the first time ever, St Botolph's had been on the verge of winning the Mereside Borough Junior Cup, and *he* had messed it all up. Now he'd have to wait another two weeks for the replay to make good.

As he plodded slowly home, he kept reliving the moment when the ball had crashed into the net. There was Danny, standing waiting for the ball. Just a little push, that was all it had needed. But he hadn't pushed it, had he? He'd kicked it.

Hard! Gary knew their number 2 hadn't touched it. He could still feel the thud as his toe made contact. Over and over, in cruel slow-motion, he saw the ball sailing past Danny's reaching fingers.

Go over the bar, he'd thought, willing the ball higher. Let it be a corner!

But his prayers had gone unanswered. It wasn't a corner. It was a goal. A brilliant goal! If only he'd scored it at the right end!

Home at last, Gary turned the key in the lock and pushed the front door open. The house was silent. His mum must have got held up at the office again. Gary was relieved. He hadn't been looking forward to telling her what had happened.

He tossed his kit-bag down in the corner and went upstairs. Of course, he knew what his mum would have said if she *had* been in. "Never mind, love" and "I'm sure you did your best" and –

perhaps worst of all – "It's not the end of the world". He hated it when she tried to cheer him up. He'd let the side down. He'd scored the equalizing goal – for the other side. And him the captain! For Gary, it *was* the end of the world.

Slamming his bedroom door shut behind him, he threw himself on to his bed and lay there staring up at the ceiling. He remembered the look on Danny's face as he realized how fast the ball was coming at him. Gary closed his eyes. But the face wouldn't go away.

"I never even said sorry," he muttered to himself.

The clock in the hall chimed six. Gary sat up. On any other day, this would have been the signal for him to change into his football strip and head up to the rec.

They probably won't bother this evening, he thought.

All round him, the football heroes he

had pinned to the wall stared back accusingly.

Scored an own goal, they seemed to be taunting. *And he didn't even say sorry.*

Perhaps they *will* be there, Gary thought, as he swung his feet down on to the carpet. I ought to go and see. Try and make it up to Danny somehow. I could lend him *Shoot Out*. He'd like that...

He jumped up, changed into jeans and sweatshirt and, with the new computer disk in his back pocket and his football under his arm, raced downstairs. There, he scribbled a note to say where he was going, grabbed a packet of crisps and left by the back door. Now he'd decided what to do, he didn't want to risk bumping into his mum. She'd only insist he had a "proper" tea.

Five minutes later, Gary was standing at the gates of the rec. He looked round. Apart from a couple of younger

kids playing on the swings, it was deserted.

Perhaps they're just late, he thought. I'll give them a couple of minutes.

He threw the ball down, and began dribbling it across the grass. He ran faster, chipping the ball past this player. That player. They fell to the ground like skittles. It was as if the ball was glued to his feet. No one could take it away from him. No one could stop him. And all around, the crowd roared him on.

"Gary! Gary! Gary!"

He dummied to the left, and sprinted forwards. The goalie could only stare in horror as he closed in for the kill. Gary glanced up, tapped the ball with his left foot, lined himself up and...

"*No!*" he screamed.

The ball, miskicked, missed by a mile. But Gary didn't notice. He stopped and stared at the wall, mouth open.

"How could he?" he muttered. He

clenched his teeth and swallowed back the tears. "How *could* he?"

Using the bar of the goal as the line on a page, a message had been neatly sprayed in bright red aerosol paint. Gary read it. Re-read it. His anger grew.

"You couldn't say it to my face, could you?" he snarled. "You dirty, rotten ... *chicken*!"

The word echoed round the park. The kids on the swings looked up, and Gary heard the sound of giggling. Perhaps they'd already seen it. Pretty soon, everyone else would see it too. He'd be a laughing stock!

Gary bent down and began digging in the earth with his fingers. If he could cover the message with mud for now, he'd be able to come back some time later and scrub it off. The trouble was, it hadn't rained for ages, and the ground was rock hard. He pulled up a handful of grass instead and tried rubbing at the letters. But it was hopeless. As he stood back, the message was still there for all the world to see.

GARY CONNELL – IS A MORONE!

Chapter 4

When Craig and Danny walked into the team changing room the following afternoon, the whole place went silent. Danny felt eighteen pairs of eyes staring at him.

"What is it?" he said. He felt his stomach churning. "Look, you can't blame me for what happened yesterday," he said. "I couldn't possibly have saved that shot."

Still no one said a word. Wesley Hunter sniggered behind his hand.

"What is it?" Danny said again.

It was Craig who first noticed the

blackboard. Screwed to the far wall, it was used by their coach – Mr Talbot – to plan match tactics. Not that that was what it was being used for now. Craig tapped Danny on the arm, and nodded towards it. A ripple of laughter ran round the room. Danny turned and stared in disbelief.

There, in yellow chalk, was a message. Short, sweet and nasty.

DANNY THOMPSON IS A CHICKEN!

Danny felt the colour draining from his face. His scalp prickled. He looked round at the grinning circle of faces.

"Who wrote that?" he asked furiously.

Gary folded his arms and leant back against the wall. "I did," he said. "What are you going to do about it?"

The room went quiet again.

"You?" said Danny, puzzled. "*You!* After what you did yesterday... Why?"

"Don't come it, Danny. You know why," said Gary.

"I don't!"

"You're lying."

"I am not lying," Danny shouted, and made a move towards Gary. Craig grabbed his arm.

"Just ignore it," he said quietly.

Gary turned round to the rest of the boys and smirked. "Of course, he would deny it, wouldn't he?" he said. "Being a chicken!" he added, and he clucked like a broody hen.

This was too much for Danny. He pulled his arm free and threw himself across the room at his tormentor. Crashing into Gary, he dragged him from the bench, and the pair of them tumbled to the floor, where they struggled furiously, each trying to pin the other down.

Instantly, everyone else in the changing room leapt to their feet. They all formed a circle round the fighting couple as Gary and Danny rolled over and over across the floor; now one on top, now the other.

"Come on, Gary!" someone shouted.

"Smack him, Danny!" yelled someone else.

The class was in uproar, and egged on by the sound of the cheering, jeering voices, both Danny and Gary redoubled their efforts to beat the other. They sprawled around on the concrete floor, arms and legs thrashing wildly. They pulled themselves up and threw wild punches.

Then Gary got the upper hand. Somehow, he managed to get Danny in a tight head-lock, and twisted him down on to his knees. The next instant, Danny managed to squirm free. He shoved Gary's chest hard with the heel of his hand and, while Gary was staggering backwards, scrambled hurriedly back to

his feet. He was half up when Gary roared and threw himself at Danny's legs. They fell back together and slammed hard into the central row of lockers.

For a second, the lockers hovered at a crazy angle – the next second gravity took over, and they fell to the floor with an almighty crash. Maurice Meacham only just avoided being crushed.

"Those two really are something!" he muttered angrily. "Not happy with throwing away the cup, now they're..."

His snidey comment went unfinished. Before the resounding crash of the fallen lockers had died away, the side-door burst open. It was Mr Talbot – half changed for the team practice – standing there in his shorts, shirt-tails and one sock. Nobody laughed as he stalked furiously across the room.

"What do you two boys think you're doing?" he bellowed. He seized them both by their shirt collars and pulled them apart. Gary and Danny glared at one another.

"He started it," Danny mumbled.

"I'm not interested in who started it," said Mr Talbot. "Good heavens. Don't you two think you've done enough already?"

"Too right," Luke Edwards whispered to Wesley Hunter.

"I've a good mind to drop both of you from the team," Mr Talbot went on.

"Yeah," Wesley whispered back to Luke. "Boot the pair of them out. They're both useless anyway."

Mr Talbot paused. He looked at the two boys in turn. "If you're going to win that cup, you must play as a team," he said. "And a team," he added, fixing his gaze on Gary, "means eleven players. Not just one. A captain must understand that – if he is to remain captain. Do you read me?"

Gary hung his head. "Sir," he said.

Behind them, Luke Edwards commented to Wesley Hunter that if Gary could read as well as he played football, then probably not.

Mr Talbot rounded on the pair of them furiously. "*Will* you two stop whispering and giggling!" he boomed. "I didn't notice *you* doing much scoring yesterday, Luke. And as for you, Wesley, I've seen trained dogs defending better. It was a miserable performance." He pulled himself up. "Now. I want these lockers stood up, then all of you outside. Three laps of the field." He turned back to Gary and Danny. "And if I hear so much as a peep out of either of you for the rest of the session, you can both go and see Mr Lawson. OK?"

"Yes, sir," they said meekly.

The thought of being sent to their headmaster filled the two boys with horror. Mr Lawson had a reputation for coming down hard on boys caught fighting. Detentions, 200-word essays entitled "Why I must not fight in school" and – worst of all – letters to parents. Neither Gary nor Danny wanted any of that.

And yet, outside at last, when Gary overtook Danny on the far side of the pitch, he couldn't resist having a final go.

"Chicken," he whispered in Danny's ear. "Mwaaaaa. Cluck. Cluck. Cluck," he went, as he sped off ahead.

Furious, Danny sprinted after him. He lunged forward and made a grab for Gary's shirt. At that moment Gary happened to glance round. Instead of seizing the thick material, Danny found himself clutching Gary's ear.

Even better! he thought, and gave it a sharp tug and twist.

With a yelp of pain, Gary lost his balance and came crashing to the ground. Danny immediately jumped on to Gary's chest and tried to pin his arms down with his knees. Gary's knee came up and hammered into Danny's stomach. Winded, he gasped for air. His eyes filled with water. Gary didn't wait for him to recover. He rolled over, jumped up, and leapt for Danny's throat. Danny raised his hands defensively. Gary kept coming. He couldn't stop. The next moment Danny's middle finger went up Gary's left nostril. Gary yowled with pain.

He was still yowling when the air was abruptly filled with another noise. It was the sound of a whistle being blown repeatedly, furiously. Mr Talbot came pounding across the field towards them.

"STOP THIS AT ONCE!" he roared. He strode the last few metres and glared down. "Gary Connell and Danny Thompson," he said. "Again! I do *not* believe it." He breathed in slowly. Both Gary and Danny knew what was coming next. They weren't wrong.

"Get changed," he barked. "Then go and stand outside Mr Lawson's office."

With their faces to the wall, Danny and Gary stood on opposite sides of the corridor waiting for the headmaster to call them in. Gary shuffled his feet nervously. It wasn't the first time he'd been sent to see Mr Lawson.

"This is all your fault," he hissed.

"Mine?" Danny whispered back. "You called me a chicken."

"You called me a moron," Gary replied hotly.

"I did not," said Danny.

"You did!"

"I didn't!"

"You did!"

Their voices were getting louder.

"When?" Danny demanded.

"You know when," Gary countered.

"I do not!" Danny shouted.

Gary turned round. "Shut up!" he

hissed. "We're in enough trouble as it is."

Danny bit his tongue. He knew Gary was right. Those sent to stand outside the head's office were expected to do so in silence. That was the rule. And he was a stickler for rules, was Mr Lawson.

The thing was, even though Danny knew it would only make matters worse if he was caught talking, he couldn't stay silent. He simply couldn't.

"Just tell me what you think I've done," he whispered.

Gary didn't reply.

"Tell me!" Danny demanded.

And as Gary finally explained about the message above the painted goalposts, Danny listened in disbelief. No wonder Gary was angry. It was a mean thing to do. But it had nothing to do with him.

"I didn't even go up the rec yesterday," he said.

Gary snorted.

"I didn't! I couldn't," he added. "Not after what happened."

There was a moment of silence. Finally Gary spoke. "I don't believe you," he said.

"Why not?" Danny shouted and spun round.

"Because it was in your writing!" Gary shouted back, and turned to face him. "You were too chicken to say it to my face yesterday, and you're too chicken to admit it now. I hate you, Danny Thompson. You're pathetic!"

"And you're a stupid—"

At that moment, the door burst open. Gary and Danny spun back to look at the wall.

"I believe you are both acquainted with the rule concerning silence," Mr Lawson said quietly.

Both boys shuffled about awkwardly. That was the worst thing about Mr Lawson – he never lost his cool. When he was angry, he spoke softly – and the angrier he got, the softer his voice became, until it was little more than an icy whisper. And when Mr Lawson started whispering, you *knew* you were for it.

"Gary," he said, his voice deathly quiet. "Follow me into my office. Daniel. Wait here. I shall deal with you later."

Chapter 5

Mr Lawson listened to Gary's story carefully. A strict stickler for rules he may have been, but he was also fair. He knew that although sticks and stones could indeed break bones, words could be just as painful.

"And you're positive that Daniel wrote the message?" he said.

"It was in his writing, sir," said Gary. "Anyway, he had the biggest reason ... what with the goal and—"

"I doubt whether the others in the team were any too pleased with you," Mr Lawson interrupted quietly.

Gary looked away. "S'pose not," he mumbled.

Mr Lawson paused. "I thought you and Daniel were friends," he said.

"So did I," said Gary angrily.

"Hmmm," said Mr Lawson thoughtfully. He had never taken Daniel Thompson for the sort of boy to tell lies. He looked up. "Is there anything else you wish to say?"

Gary shook his head.

"In that case," he said. "You may go. Send Daniel in, please. And wait for me in the corridor."

As the door swung open, Danny looked up.

"Your turn," said Gary.

"How was it?" Danny mouthed.

Gary scowled, and ran his finger across his throat. Danny gulped. He knew that all he could do was tell the truth. But what if Mr Lawson didn't believe him? After all, Gary hadn't.

It was impossible to tell *what* Mr Lawson was thinking as he listened to the second version of the story. Only when Danny had finished did he finally speak.

"And you give me your word you did not write the message," he said.

"On my life!" Danny exclaimed. "I didn't. I wouldn't..."

"But Gary said it was written in your handwriting."

Danny shrugged. "I s'pose whoever did it must have wanted it to look as if I wrote it."

Mr Lawson sighed. "Go and get Gary," he said.

He didn't like this sort of situation. He suspected that Daniel was right – that someone else *was* involved. And if that was the case, then their reactions had been understandable. However – and it was, for Mr Lawson, a big however – that did not in any way excuse their behaviour. He would not tolerate brawling in his school.

It was four o'clock before Mr Lawson finished with the two boys. Gary set off at once on his bike. Craig was waiting for Danny at the school gates.

"So, what happened?" he said at once.

"Well," said Danny. "For a start, we've both got to stay behind after school on Friday..."

"And?"

Danny groaned. "He's writing to our parents."

"Oh, what?" said Craig. "Your dad's going to go berserk!"

"I know," said Danny.

"You're bound to be grounded."

"I know," said Danny.

"For a week, at least. Maybe two... And that'll mean missing United at home."

"I *know*!" he snapped. He turned away and stomped off along the pavement.

Craig ran to catch him up. "Sorry," he said. "I didn't mean to rub it in."

Danny shrugged. He didn't slacken his pace. And when he got to the T-junction, rather than turning right towards the estate, he turned abruptly to the left.

"Where are you going?" asked Craig.

"Gary said there's some message been

written up the rec," he called back. "He reckons I wrote it. I'm going to have a look."

"Up the rec?" Craig said, as he trotted behind Danny. "But I didn't think you went there yesterday."

"I didn't," said Danny. "That's what I kept telling him."

"And what did it say, this message?" asked Craig.

Danny sniggered. "Something about him being a moron!"

"A moron!" Craig laughed. "Well, he is!"

"I know!" he said, and swallowed. "He's a cretin!"

"An idiot!"

"A brain like a stegosaurus," said Danny.

"A brain like a banana!" said Craig.

"Ba-na-na Brain!" they both growled together, and began laughing all over again.

As they walked through the gates of the rec, and Danny saw the streak of red above the painted crossbar, he stopped laughing. He chewed the inside of his mouth. They continued walking over the pitch. Halfway across, the words suddenly stood out. Danny froze to the spot. His heart was racing.

"It does *look* like your writing," said Craig slowly.

"I can see that," said Danny. "I suppose you don't believe me now either."

"That's not what I said," said Craig. "But. . ."

Danny turned on him. "Look, loads of people do their A's like triangles," he said angrily.

He walked closer to the splash of graffiti. The thing was, everything about the writing was familiar. The triangular A's, the loopy L's, the backward Y. Danny found himself wondering whether he *had* written it after all!

Perhaps he was losing his marbles and had done it without knowing. Perhaps he'd sleepwalked there in the middle of the night.

"If *you* didn't write it..." Craig began.

"I didn't!" Danny shouted. "Apart from anything else, I know how to spell 'moron'."

"OK, OK!" said Craig. "The thing is, whoever *did* write it wanted to make it look as if you'd done it."

Danny nodded. "That's what I said to Mr Lawson."

"The question is," Craig went on, "why?"

"I've been thinking about that, too," said Danny. "You remember when we voted for who should be captain?"

Craig nodded. "You proposed Gary. I seconded him," he said. "And he won easily."

"Yeah," said Danny. "But not unanimously. There were three votes against. What if one of those three is using the Eastfields match as an excuse to get rid of Gary as captain..."

"And become captain himself!" Craig exclaimed.

"Exactly," said Danny. "So who voted against?"

"There was Maurice," said Craig slowly.

"And Wesley," said Danny.

"And Luke Edwards," they both said together.

"But which one do you think it is?" said Craig.

"That,'" said Danny grimly, "is what I intend to find out."

Chapter 6

"Come on," said Craig, turning to go. "There's nothing more we can do here."

At that moment, a voice rang out from the far end of the rec. Danny looked round. It was Gary. He was on his bike and pedalling furiously towards them. Hanging from the handlebars was a small tin of paint; in his hand was a brush.

"Returned to the scene of the crime, eh?" he said as he skidded to a halt next to them. He glared at Danny. "You've got a nerve, coming here," he said.

"It's a free country," said Craig.

"Who asked you?" said Gary angrily. He turned back to Danny. "You still reckon you didn't write it?"

"I didn't!" said Danny.

Gary turned away in disgust. "You make me sick," he said as he unhooked the handle of the paint pot, let his bike clatter to the grass, and strode over to the wall. "Chicken!"

Danny bit his lip. "Look," he said, as he followed him. "If I was a chicken, I'd have disguised my writing, wouldn't I?"

Gary hesitated. He could see the logic in what Danny was saying.

"Well, wouldn't I?" Danny persisted.

"Who did write it, then?" said Gary, as he crouched down and levered the lid off the pot with his penknife.

"That's what we've got to find out," said Danny.

Gary dipped his brush into the thick yellow paint. He wiped the excess drips off on the side of the tin, and walked over to the wall. Unfortunately, even though he stretched up as high as he could, the letters were just out of reach. He turned round.

"I need a bunk up," he said.

Danny and Craig remained where they were. Danny folded his arms. "Not until you say you believe me."

Gary stared at him. His fists clenched and unclenched. "All right," he said finally. "I believe you."

"*And* apologize for what you put on the blackboard," Danny added.

Gary didn't answer.

"I'm waiting," said Danny.

But Gary was no longer looking at him. He was staring back towards the entrance gates where twenty or so boys and girls had just come running into the rec. Danny and Craig turned to see what had caught his attention. As the kids got nearer, Danny realized that they were all from their class.

"What are they doing here?" said Craig.

"As if you didn't know!" Gary shouted. "You rotten—"

"I didn't tell anyone," Danny protested. "Except Craig."

"And *I* didn't," said Craig hurriedly, as the other two turned on him. "How could I?"

"Well, someone did!" Gary yelled.

"Yeah!" said Danny. "Whoever wrote the message in the first place."

Gary stared at him for a second. Then he glanced back at the advancing horde. They were making so much noise – whooping and whistling – that all the other kids in the park were abandoning their games and joining in. Something was going on, and they wanted to know what.

"Come on," said Danny, bending down. "Climb up on my back. Let's get that wall painted quick."

Gary didn't argue. He did not want the others seeing the message. By the time the first of the kids were close enough to read the words, MORONE had already disappeared under a thick coat of yellow paint. Seeing what was happening, a loud cry of disappointment went up.

"Gary Connell is a what?" somebody yelled.

"A half-wit!" someone else replied.

"A loser!" said Wesley Hunter.

"A captain who scores for the other side!" Maurice Meacham suggested, and the sound of taunting laughter filled the air.

Ignoring them, Danny slowly crawled along the bottom of the wall, while Gary painted out the remaining words.

"So, what did it say, Danny?" Luke Edwards called out.

"Yeah, tell us!" came a chorus of voices.

"What's the point of getting us all up here if you're not going to tell us?"

Gary froze. "So you *did* tell them," he said.

"I didn't," Danny said weakly. Once again the situation was getting out of control. He twisted his head round and looked up at Gary. "Honest, I didn't."

Without a word, Gary painted out the last two remaining letters. The message had gone. But not his anger. As he stepped down, he dipped his brush into the paint one last time. Then, before Danny could straighten up, Gary slapped the thick yellow goo, splat, down on Danny's head and ran the brush right the way down the length of his back.

Danny leapt up. "What do you think you're playing at?" he screamed, and shoved Gary back against the wall.

"Whassup?" Gary jeered, and dunked the brush in the paint again. He held it up menacingly in front of him. "Want a yellow belly as well?"

Danny rubbed at the back of his head. His hair was covered in the slimy paint. He looked at his hand.

"You're round the twist!" he yelled. "If I'd written it I'd have known what it said. And if I knew, I could have told them at school. Why bring them all up here?"

"Yeah, very clever!" Gary sneered. "You've got all the answers, haven't you? Almost had me fooled." He turned to the others. "He reckons one of you lot did it."

The group of boys and girls reacted with an angry rumble of indignation.

"Oh, yeah – who?" someone said.

"Typical!" said somebody else.

Danny stared round helplessly at the angry faces. There was nothing he could do or say.

"Why don't you just clear off?" said

Gary. "You're not welcome here. And you too," he said, turning on Craig.

"But…" Craig began.

"Go on," said Gary. "Hop it!"

Danny and Craig looked at each other. They had no other choice. Heads down, they walked away. The sound of booing and hissing rang in their ears. It was like being at a pantomime – and *they* were the wicked villains.

They were on the far side of the rec before either boy spoke.

"I'm sorry," said Danny finally. "I didn't want you to…"

"It's OK," said Craig. "It'll blow over." He sighed. "You know, the more I think about this, the more clever it is. All three of us are being set up."

"How do you mean?" asked Danny.

"Well, think about it. We agreed who made sure Gary got to be captain, didn't we?"

"Yeah," said Danny. "You and me."

Craig nodded. "But he's not going to stay captain for long if he's not careful, is he? You heard what Mr Talbot said. I reckon he's already thinking about making a change. And if he does, who takes over?"

Danny shrugged. "It *should* have been me. Or you," he added, and grinned.

"Right," said Craig. "But not any more. Whoever wrote that message about Gary has managed to get all three of us into trouble. And anyway, who'd vote for you or me now?"

Danny shook his head sadly. The sound of distant booing was still echoing round the park. "No one," he said.

"Right again," said Craig. "And do you know the worst of it?" he said. "By copying your handwriting, the person who *did* write it has managed to split the three of us up."

As they reached the gates, Danny glanced round at the angry crowd of kids. Gary was leading a chant of "Off! Off! Off!" He sighed. Craig was right. Whoever had written that first mischief-making message above the goalposts hadn't had to do anything else since. Gary had done it all for him. And that *was* clever!

"Which means," Craig went on. "That we'll end up with Maurice as captain. . ."

"Or Wesley. . ."

"Or Luke Edwards!" they said together, and groaned.

The two boys walked on in silence. The nearer to home Danny got, the more nervous he felt. It wasn't helped by the curious stares he kept getting from everyone they passed.

"Does it really look that bad?" he asked.

Craig slowed and looked up and down Danny's back. "Yes," he said.

"Oh, blimey!" Danny moaned. "Mum

is going to go mad! And then they're going to get that letter tomorrow..." He looked round. "Craig," he said. "Do me a favour, will you?"

"What?" said Craig. "Get you a plane ticket to Mexico?"

"Not quite," Danny smiled. "I know this sounds a bit soft but... Come back to the house with me. I think I'm going to need all the support I can get."

Craig looked at his friend. He knew what Danny's parents could be like when they were angry – and there was no doubt that they were going to be very angry indeed. A mate's a mate, and all that, but there were limits! Danny caught the expression on his face and laughed.

"I'm sorry," said Craig. "Anything else, but..."

"It's all right," said Danny. "I've had a better idea anyway. I'll go round to my grandad's. He'll know what to do."

Chapter 7

"Danny!" his grandad exclaimed as he opened the door. "What a lovely surprise. Come in, come in and... Oh, dear!" He stared at Danny's hair. "Been doing a spot of DIY?"

Danny turned round and showed him the streak of yellow paint down his back. Grandad tutted. "This looks serious," he said. "What have you been up to?"

"It's a long story," Danny muttered.

"I dare say it is," his grandad replied, and sighed. "Right then. Give me your sweatshirt. I'll stick it in a bucket to soak – lucky it's only emulsion paint. Then go

and wash your hair. And I'll call your mother to let her know where you are. OK?"

"OK, Grandad," said Danny. And as he ran up the stairs, he realized he felt better already. Grandad Thompson had a way of taking control. Often, it could be a pain in the neck. But sometimes – like now – it felt wonderful.

By the time he'd rinsed his hair for the third time, most of the paint had gone. Downstairs again, he sat on a kitchen chair while his grandad stood behind him, removing the bits that had dried with a fine toothcomb.

"It's a good job you keep it so short, otherwise we'd never have got it all out." He snorted. "Not like your father at your age. Long, lank and greasy, his hair was. Absolutely horrible. And could I get him to have it cut? Could I heck! I remember once..."

Danny smiled. He liked hearing about

his dad – particularly stories of when he'd been in trouble.

"There, that ought to do," said his grandad at last, and he lay the comb down on the table. "Brush the bits off into the sink. That's it. Right, now, are you hungry?"

Danny shook his head.

"Thirsty? Would you like some squash?"

"No, thanks," said Danny.

Grandad nodded. "OK, then," he said, sitting himself down at the kitchen table. "Why don't you start at the beginning."

And that was exactly what Danny did. He told his grandad everything. About the football match, the graffiti, the fights in the changing room and on the football pitch, about Mr Lawson and the letters to his parents... Absolutely everything.

"And it wasn't my fault!" he blurted out, as his story came to an end. "I didn't do anything! And the worst of it is, if we don't sort ourselves out – as a team – we're never going to win the cup. And we've got to!"

Danny's grandad stroked his chin thoughtfully. "And you definitely didn't write on the wall about Gary?" he said.

"No, Grandad," said Danny, looking straight into his eyes. "I swear I didn't."

The old man nodded. "And he called you a chicken, eh?"

"*And* wrote it on the blackboard!" Danny said. "When I get my hands on him, I'll—"

The old man cut him short. "Not a good idea, Danny," he said. "Not a good idea at all. That's the way wars start. No. What we need here is a lasting truce, not an escalation of the conflict." He grinned mischievously. "And I think I've got just the solution. The Chicken and the Egg."

Danny stared at his grandad. "The

Chicken and the Egg?" he repeated. "What's that?"

Grandad smiled. "It's a long story," he said, his eyes twinkling. "A long time ago," he began. "When I was a little bit younger than you are now, we had a situation very much like this in the street where I lived."

"What?" said Danny. "Someone called you a chicken?"

"No, not me," said Grandad. "A boy called Cyril Tucker. But it was my grandfather who sorted it all out. Now *there* was a wise old man. You'd have loved him, Danny. Anyway," he said, taking a deep breath. "It was all a mis-understanding. A boy called Walter something-or-other called Cyril a chicken – for something he hadn't done."

"Just like me," said Danny.

"Cyril attacked."

"Just like me!"

"Walter counter-attacked."

Danny grinned. "Just like Gary," he said.

"Cyril counter-counter-attacked," his grandad said. "And so it went on!"

"Just like us!" Danny laughed.

"Oh, far worse," his grandad said. "It turned really nasty. I remember one afternoon, Walter went into Cyril's house – we never locked them up in those days – and emptied the feathers from two pillows all over Mrs Tucker's parlour.

She went mad! Then Cyril set fire to Walter's cap and blazer. Then Walter and a couple of his friends grabbed Cyril after school and wrote CHICKEN across his forehead in indelible ink. Then Cyril..." He paused. "In short, it all got completely out of hand."

Danny sat, open-mouthed. It was odd to think of his grandfather as a boy, and odder still to hear that Grandad had been in the middle of a situation so like his own.

"And, of course," he continued, "in those days, we all played out in the road. Hardly any cars, you see. So you couldn't afford to fall out with anyone. After all, everyone knew everyone else. You had to see them every day. That's how Grandfather got involved. He knew what was going on; and he came up with a plan to sort things out, once and for all."

"The Chicken and the Egg," said Danny.

"Precisely," said Grandad, and chuckled.

"So what *is* it?" asked Danny.

"Patience," his grandad said. "That's what I'm just coming to."

As Danny listened to his grandad's explanation, a grin spread slowly over his face. The plan was a gem.

"It's perfect!" he said finally. "But why should Gary go along with it?"

"Greed," he replied simply.

"And what if he guesses...?"

"He won't," said Grandad. "No one ever does. Trust me."

Chapter 8

At half past ten the following morning, Danny and Craig were up the rec again, slowly cycling over the grass.

"The thing is," Danny was saying, "Grandad reckons that you've got the most important job. It's up to you to explain the ground rules so clearly that there can't be any misunderstandings afterwards. You did phone Gary, didn't you?"

Craig nodded. "It's all set. He'll be here at eleven."

"Good," said Danny. "Now, are you sure you know what you've got to say?"

"I think so," said Craig. "Let's just run through it one more time."

"I can do better than that," said Danny. "Grandad wrote down the main points. Here," he said, pulling a folded piece of paper from his kit-bag and handing it to Craig. "Read through this."

At eleven on the dot, Gary arrived. He jumped off his bike and strode up to the other two.

"So what's this all about?" he said. "You made it sound important."

"It is," said Craig, as he slipped the list of instructions into his back pocket. "The thing is, you and Danny have reached an impasse," he said, quoting from the notes.

"A what?" said Gary.

"Stalemate," said Danny.

"This all started because you wouldn't believe that Danny didn't write that graffiti," said Craig. "Now, since he can't prove he didn't, and since we can't make you change your mind, we've ... errm, devised a plan to effect a lasting truce."

"I wish you'd speak English," said Gary angrily.

"We've got to stop being enemies!" said Danny. "It's not getting us anywhere—"

"Yeah, well if you hadn't—"

Craig raised his hands and called for quiet. "The name of the plan," he announced, "is the Chicken and the Egg."

Gary grinned. "Sounds appropriate," he said.

"Exactly," said Craig. "Since you accused Danny of being a chicken, it is right and proper that he should use eggs to bring the situation to a fitting conclusion."

Danny reached into his bag and pulled out an egg box. He flipped open the lid and revealed two eggs nestling inside. Gary looked at them and sniggered.

"What are they for?" he said.

"That's what I'm about to tell you," said Craig. "Now listen, and listen carefully."

"Go on, then," said Gary.

"The offer is this," he said. "Danny will give you ten pounds if you let him break two eggs on your head."

Gary stared at him and Danny in amazement. "You two must think I'm mental!" he said. "Why should I agree to that?"

"Ten pounds?" said Danny.

Gary fell silent.

"The thing is," said Craig. "If you decide to go ahead, you must agree that this marks the end of all hostilities."

Gary looked at Danny and shrugged. "He's at it again," he said.

"He means that whatever happens, after this, we're quits," said Danny.

"For the following reasons," Craig added, remembering the notes he had memorized. "One. By suggesting this meeting, Danny is not acting behind your back, but rather the opposite. And if you choose to accept his offer..." He laughed. "On your head be it!"

"And if I don't?" said Gary.

"He's still proved that he's not a chicken," said Craig. "Two. If you *do* say yes, Danny will have got his own back for what you did yesterday with the paint, and agrees not to take the matter any further. Don't you, Danny?"

Danny rubbed his hand over his head. Bits of the hardened paint that Grandad had missed were still clinging stubbornly to his hair. He'd need a haircut to get rid of all of it.

"Don't you?" Craig repeated.

Danny looked up and nodded. "Yeah," he said. "But I still think he's getting the better deal."

"Three," Craig continued. "The ten pounds..."

"Yeah, yeah," said Gary. "The ten pounds is the carrot, I know. To make me agree." He stared at Craig. "What's the trick?" he said.

Keeping his face straight, Craig merely repeated the offer. "Danny will give you ten pounds if you let him break two eggs on your head."

"Where's the ten pounds?" said Gary suspiciously.

Danny pulled out a crisp tenner from his back pocket and held it out for Gary to inspect.

"And it's not a forgery?"

"Course it's not," said Danny irritably. "My grandad gave it to me this morning."

Gary paced around the grass thoughtfully. It seemed foolproof. And since he'd had his pocket money stopped for a month because of the letter that had arrived from Mr Lawson that morning, the ten pounds would certainly come in handy.

In the meantime, other kids in the park had noticed Gary, Craig and Danny deep in conversation. Given the fun and games of the previous evening, they decided to go and investigate. And when Luke Edwards and Maurice Meacham rolled up on their bikes and saw something was going on, they rode over too.

"What's happening?" Luke asked a girl in the crowd.

"That boy," she said, pointing to Danny, "is going to give that boy ten pounds if he lets him smash two eggs on his head."

Luke smiled. "Is he now?" he said. He was puzzled but, like everyone else, stayed to find out what would happen next.

"Well?" said Craig.

Gary stopped and looked up. He'd

gone through the offer a hundred times in his head. Whichever way he looked at it, he was going to end up ten quid better off. How could he lose? He looked Craig in the face.

"All right," he said. "You're on."

Craig smiled. "Good decision," he said. "Now, before we start you've both got to agree that whatever the outcome, neither of you will take any further action whatsoever."

Danny and Gary stared at one another. They nodded.

"Shake on it then," said Craig.

Danny stuck his hand out. Gary paused for a second, before seizing it with his own hand.

"Right," said Craig. "Gary. Kneel down. Danny. Take the two eggs and stand behind him."

The crowd of children whispered and giggled as Danny and Gary took up their positions. Craig looked at his watch.

"It is eleven-thirty," he announced. "Let the Chicken and the Egg commence."

The boys and girls went silent. Danny looked down at the two eggs, one in his right hand, one in his left. He stared from one to the other, as if trying to decide which to use first. Meanwhile, Gary looked ahead, wincing in anticipation.

Suddenly, the waiting was over. With a flick of his wrist, Danny brought the right-hand egg down on Gary's head. A cheer went up as the shell smashed. It was followed by squeals of laughter and disgust as slimy white and gooey yolk trickled down over Gary's forehead and cheeks. One stray blob slithered down the back of his neck.

Gary screwed his face up, but continued to stare ahead. It wasn't *that* bad, he thought. One down, one to go. Normally, if he wanted extra money for

something, he had to earn it. Wash the car, mow the lawn; that sort of thing. This was going to be the easiest ten pounds he'd ever made.

And yet, as one or two in the crowd began to snigger knowingly, Gary began to have the horrible feeling that he'd missed something. He shuffled about uncomfortably on his knees.

"Come on, then," he said. "Get it over with."

Danny didn't reply. And when he looked round, Gary saw that both he and Craig were trying their best not to laugh.

"The second egg," he said angrily. "Are you going to break it on my head, or what?"

"No," said Danny, simply. "No, I'm not."

The laughter from the crowd of children increased. One by one, those who hadn't understood what was going on had it explained to them by those who had. Finally, Gary was the only person who still didn't understand.

"Go on!" he shouted. "That was the deal."

"No it wasn't," someone yelled out.

"The offer was that Danny would give you ten pounds if you let him break two eggs on your head," Craig said. "*Two* eggs."

"I know that," said Gary. "And I did let him." He twisted round to Danny. "So, get on with it."

"No," Danny repeated. "I only feel like breaking *one* egg."

Suddenly, Gary clicked. He leapt up, furious. "You tricked me," he screamed as he lunged at Danny.

But Craig was ready for him. He grabbed Gary's arm and, with a couple of volunteers from the crowd, held him back.

"You agreed not to do anything else,"

Craig reminded him. "Whatever the outcome!"

Gary continued to struggle furiously. But it was hopeless, there was no way he could break free.

"Anyway," said Danny. "You weren't tricked. You were outwitted."

Gary stopped wriggling and stared at Danny. Then at Craig. He knew they were right. It was his fault for letting the promise of the money get in the way. They'd told him everything – but he just hadn't seen it. The whole thing was clever. Very clever. Suddenly, his face broke into a huge grin.

"You got me, didn't you?" he said.

"Fair and square," said Danny. "Truce?"

Gary nodded. "Truce," he said.

Once again, a cheer went up from the crowd of spectators. Gary took the towel that Danny pulled from his bag and rubbed it over his head, and round his face and neck. Then he turned to the cheering crowd and bowed.

Only one person seemed unhappy by the outcome. He glared at the three boys – friends once more – with a mixture of anger and regret.

"You really *are* a morone, aren't you?" he called out.

Gary looked round. It was Luke Edwards. "What did you say?"

"You heard," said Luke.

"A mor-one," said Gary slowly. "With an 'e'?"

Luke turned bright red. He knew he'd made a fatal mistake.

"Yeah. I mean, that's what Danny called you, isn't it? S'what he sprayed on the wall. That's what I heard," he blustered. "I mean, that's what he told me."

With each word, Luke was landing himself deeper and deeper in it. If only he'd kept his mouth shut!

"It was *you*!" Gary yelled.

"Me, what?" Luke said, backing nervously out of the crowd.

"*You* wrote it!" said Gary. "You started all this. YOU!"

"I told you," Danny said to Craig.

"Where's that other egg?" Gary roared.

"Here," said Danny.

Seeing what was about to happen, Luke turned on his heels and raced off. Gary and Craig immediately leapt on to their bikes and sped after him, with Danny – egg in hand – bringing up the rear. Luke was fast, but not fast enough to escape three boys on bikes. As he raced down the slope at the far corner, he found Craig blocking his way. He stopped. Danny skidded to a halt to his right; Gary, to his left.

The three of them dismounted and advanced towards him. Luke hesitated. Suddenly, he made a dash for it. At least, he tried to. The next instant he tripped over Craig's outstretched leg and ended up sprawling on the grass.

Gary was on him at once. He rolled him over and pinned his arms down with his knees. Luke tried kicking him, but Craig soon put a stop to that by sitting on his legs.

Danny approached slowly. He knelt down and clamped Luke's head still with his knees. Then he held the second egg gently against Luke's forehead.

"Oh, don't!" Luke moaned. "You've got it all wrong..."

"I don't think so," said Danny.

Gary looked up at Danny. "Go on then," he said.

"I thought you'd want to help?" Danny said.

Gary grinned. "Too right!" he said. And, with Danny and Gary pressing lightly down on the egg, Craig began the countdown.

"Ten, nine, eight, seven, six, five, four..."

The two boys increased the pressure on the egg.

"...three, two, one."

Splat!

The shell shattered. The egg splattered. Luke shuddered with revulsion as the slimy goo slid down into his eyes, his ears, his mouth.

"You creeps!" he spluttered.

Danny moved his knees apart; Gary and Craig released their grip. The three of them stood up. Luke remained where he was.

Gary stared down at him. "Now we're *all* quits," he said. "But if you ever pull a stunt like that again..."

"Let's go," said Craig quietly. "He isn't worth it."

As they wheeled their bicycles away, they passed the boys and girls who were just arriving to see what had happened.

"Is it all over?" they asked disappointedly.

"Yeah," said Craig. "All over his face!"

Danny and Gary laughed.

"What shall we do now?" said Gary.

"Why don't we spend that tenner?" Craig suggested.

"I can't," said Danny. "I just borrowed it off my grandad."

Gary looked at him. "You must have been fairly sure I'd fall for it," he said.

"*I* wasn't, but *he* was," said Danny.

"You mean you told your grandad what it was for?" said Gary.

Craig laughed. "It was *his* idea," he said.

"Actually, it was my great, great grandfather who thought it up first," said Danny.

Gary shook his head. "Well, whoever it was, it was pretty clever," he said. "I can't wait to try it out on someone else!"

They all laughed.

"So what *shall* we do now?" said Craig.

Danny stopped and reached into the kit-bag. He pulled out his football, threw it up and kicked it high in the air. He grinned.

"We haven't played Corner for a while," he said.

Gary let his bike drop. "Race you to the goal," he shouted.

Chapter 9

From his hiding place behind the pavilion, Danny's grandad watched the three boys sprinting towards the far wall and setting up their game. He hadn't caught everything that had been said that morning, but one thing was clear; Danny, Craig and Gary had patched up their differences. What was more, in the process, they'd managed to flush out the real culprit.

"Or should that be the real *bad egg*!" he chortled as he made his way home.

Two Wednesdays later, Danny's grandad was watching his grandson playing again. This time he wasn't hiding. It was the replay of the Mereside Borough Junior Cup, being held at Eastfields. He was standing on the touchline near the centre of the pitch, bellowing his support.

"Come on, St Botolph's!" he roared.

The team couldn't have played better. Passing, dribbling, attacking, defending – they were playing like true professionals. Not once did Danny find himself undefended. Not once did Gary hog the ball. In fact the only goal of the first half resulted from his cutting short a run down the left wing, and floating the ball over to Luke Edwards, who headed it soundly into the far corner of the net.

At the beginning of the second half, it looked as if Eastfields were about to equalize. Their number 2 struck a dangerously dipping shot from way outside the penalty area. It was heading for the top right corner. Danny leapt into the air, arms outstretched. The ball hurtled down. Danny flew across the goal-mouth to meet it. Would he make it?

The next instant, the ball thudded against his fingers with tremendous force. Catching it was impossible. All Danny could hope to do was push it over the bar for a corner.

As he fell down to the ground, a cheer went up around the pitch. For a second Danny feared that the goal had gone in after all. He looked up. No, he realized. It was the St Botolph's lot who were cheering. He'd done it!

"Bravo, Danny!" his grandad roared. "Well done, lad!" He turned to the man standing next to him. "That's my grandson, that is," he said proudly.

"Mr Thompson, is it?" the man said, and stuck out his hand. "The name's Talbot. The boys' football coach," he explained. "Danny's playing really well.

The whole team is. I..." He turned back to the match, where a short corner had just been intercepted by Craig. "*Go on!*" he roared.

Racing up the field, Craig passed the ball to Gary, who kicked it far up the field to a running Luke Edwards. Luke chipped it past their number 6 and floated it back towards the goal. Gary was ready and waiting. *Boof!* He booted the ball on the volley, smack bang into the middle of the net. The goalie never stood a chance.

Ten minutes before the end, Gary scored again. And Craig's goal – in the eighty-fifth minute – made it 4-0. When the final whistle blew, a deafening roar of triumph went up. St Botolph's had done it. They'd won. The Mereside Borough Junior Cup was theirs!

First on to the pitch to congratulate them was Mr Talbot, followed closely by Danny's grandad.

"Well done, lads," cried Mr Talbot. "You played a blinder. Each and every one of you. I don't know what got into you this afternoon, but that was *real* teamwork. I'm proud of you."

Danny, who along with Gary, Craig and Luke had been hoisted up on to the shoulders of his team-mates, looked down. He saw his grandad beaming up at him.

"We did it, Grandad!" he yelled.

"You certainly did," his grandad called back. He winked. "With a little bit of help."

"Yeah. I... Whooaah!" He roared with laughter as the boys carrying him abruptly lurched to the left. Swaying precariously, he turned back to his grandad. "I'll see you later," he shouted. "And thanks!"

Danny's grandad smiled as his grandson was whisked off across the playing field. "Don't thank me," he chuckled softly. "Thank the Chicken and the Egg."